The Yorkshire Eskimo And Others

Nonsense poems
By a Yorkshire man with a
weird sense of humour

Copyright © 2018

Ronald Town

Preface

I am Yorkshire born and bred and have lived in Rotherham all my life.
From my early school days I have liked poetry and in my twenties
started writing amusing monologues after listening to Albert and the
Lion and other monologues performed by Stanley Holloway. My
humble attempts were written long hand and no longer exist. After
retirement I joined a Creative Writing group on Kimberworth Park and
many of the poems included in this volume were written for our weekly
meetings.
Other poems were written after visits to friends and neighbours and I
have their permission to include these in this volume.
Most of my poems are humorous or as I call them, nonsense poems.

Many are based around the area in which I have lived all my life.
I am a retired joinery lecturer and secretary at the local church which
will explain the content of some of my work.

Acknowledgements

I would like to thank local author Jeanette Hensby and her family for
encouraging me to publish my work and for their advice on how to
accomplish this.

Also my friends and family for listening to my poems.
And Jane Bagshaw for the Yorkshire Eskimo on the front cover.

Contents

The Joys of decorating

My magic train spotter's hat

My working life

My dream Holiday

Who is the very first?

The Yorkshire time traveller

Worst Christmas presents ever

My wife's won the lottery

The eternal optimist

My keys are missing

The man who never shaves

Patron Saint

Go carts on Kimberworth Park

School days

My Sporting achievements

Bungee Jumping

The knocker up of Old Kimberworth Circa 1900

David the blacksmith

Friends

I want to live forever

Transparent Daisy and invisible Dan

In a land called Sunshine

Where the Pooch tree grows

Married Bliss

The walking group

Cherry wine and a Gladstone bag

Coming Home to Yorkshire

Coming home to Yorkshire is what I dream at nights,
I'm living now in Blackpool, and service all the lights.
I live with Uncle Wally, and live on boiled ham.
He is a local celebrity and drives a Blackpool Tram.

Coming home to Yorkshire is what I want to do.
I'm living now in Chester, and working at the zoo.
I live with Aunty Betty, and live on Eccles cakes,
She works at the gallery, and discovers all the fakes.

Coming home to Yorkshire, is my greatest desire,
I'm living now in Wigan, with a taxi cab for hire.
I live with my cousin Horace, and live on Ginger Beer,
He is a famous juggler, and performs at Wigan Pier.

Coming home to Yorkshire is one of my greatest aims,
I'm living now in Liverpool and making window frames.
I live with my second cousin and live on egg and chips,
He is the local carpenter and works on sailing ships.

Coming home to Yorkshire seems impossible to me,
I'm living now in Glasgow and selling cups of tea.
I'm living with Uncle Angus and living on haggis now,
He is a small time farmer with a horse and sheep and cow.

At last I'm back in Yorkshire; it's where my future lies,
I'm living now in Kimberworth, and painting butterflies.
I'm living with my family, and all is well and good,
I'm no longer eating rubbish, but good old Yorkshire pud.

The Yorkshire Eskimo

In the land of ice and snow
Lives a Yorkshire Eskimo.
He lives with huskies all quite tame.
This is how he grew to fame.

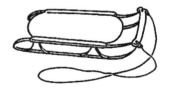

He was born in a town called Rotherham,
In a house quite near to Greasbrough dam.
William Peanut they did name him,
A name he hated and who can blame him.

He was unhappy with his lot,
Especially at times when he was hot.
But all that changed so long ago.
For his happiest time was in the snow.

He started work at fifteen, building sleds,
For a Yorkshire company in large wooden sheds.
Into his work, William put his heart and soul,
And sent his work to a warehouse at the North Pole.

He soon became the finest exponent at his game,
And overseas they spread his fame.
And finally his boss said, he'd have to let him go,
To where the Eskimos live in that land of snow.

At last he lost that stupid name,
And Billy Snowball he soon became.
He married lovely Akna of Inuit fame,
And Akna Snowball she became.

His business boomed making bespoke sleds.
Now he and Akna worked in igloo sheds.
He soon became king of them all,
That Yorkshire Eskimo, Billy Snowball.

Now Greasbrough's famous for its church and dam,
A credit indeed to fair Rotherham.
But it's most internationally famous son of all,
Is the legendary Eskimo, King Billy Snowball.

My Wardrobe

My wardrobe is full of wonder each visit brings surprise.
It's full of things long forgotten, like flares and kipper ties.
It's the story of my teenage days, a remnant of the sixties,
Of sizes belonging to a slimmer Ron, like trousers that no longer fit me.
It is a treasure trove of memories of days when quality mattered
But when trying on my sixties clothes I soon become quite shattered.

I sometimes reminisce, and clothing out I bring,
And remember those good old days, when I was a fashion King.
My velvet Jacket is long gone, along with my winkle pickers
And broad striped suits alas today are only worn by vicars.
Paisley ties are still there, along with fancy braces,
Leather belts and yellow socks, and shoes with bright red laces.

Once I chose the clothes I wore like any true Yorkshire man oughta
But now the clothes I choose are never right, too dark, too bright, too tight.
They are chosen now behind my back by my lovely wife and daughter.
For old times' sake I often wear a colourful array,
Of 70s shirts and psychedelic ties, clothes so loud they shout,
Because I can wear what I want, I'm the boss in my own house,
When my wife goes out.

My wardrobe's bursting at the seams with clothes that are too small.
But when I lose that extra stone, and a half, I'll be able to wear them all.
I'm on a diet once again and soon I'll be able to wear my treasures.
Wearing anything I want, once again, will be one of life's great pleasures.
In your dreams says my wife very much to my surprise,
Grow up Ron and chuck em out and buy some clothes your proper size.

It's the end of an era, my disappearing youth.
But she's right you know, she always is, I'll have to face the truth.
My wardrobe full of retro clothes that will never fit again,
It's all a distant memory now and it causes me such pain.
I'll have a clear out next week, and to the charity shop I'll take everything
That once made me the envy of all, the Kimberworth Park fashion King.

DIY is my game

I am a DIY expert, I tell all my friends.
As for my many skills, the list it never ends.
In our new house, every job has been done.
So I keep on boasting, to my wife and to my son

"Fix me a shelf" said the love of my life.
"And do right it now if you value your life".
"Put it in the pantry two foot from the top"
"So off you go now to the local wood shop".

So I measured the shelf twice, as they tell you to do,
And wrote in my book, nine inches wide by three foot two.
So back I came from the wood yard as pleased as can be,
To find that my shelf should have been three foot three.

My wife was not pleased, I could tell from her face,
"As a DIY expert you're simply a disgrace".
So back to the shop embarrassed I went,
Life would be simpler if we lived in a tent.

Back to the pantry with my new piece of wood,
My wife will be happy and life will be good.
My wife came to see, expecting good news,
To find I had no bearers, no plugs and no screws

Back to the shop with a flea in my ear,
I wish I was in the pub, with a pie and some beer
The jobs finally done, I'm now walking tall,
But the following day it fell of the wall.

The moral is this, is don't boast of your skill,
And when jobs need doing pretend to be ill.
Be well prepared before jobs come around,
And bury all your tools in a hole in the ground.

Pockets

Tradesmen have trousers with plenty of pockets
They put rulers in some, and in others put sockets.
If you're ever in need of a nail or a screw,
A biro or string, or a packet of lockets.
Just ask a tradesman with plenty of pockets.

In them are kept screwdrivers, and sandpaper too
Things you can read, and things you can chew
On November the fifth, if you run out of rockets,
Just send for a tradesman with some in his pockets.

Some work on a farm, and just out of habit,
Out of their trousers they'll pull out a rabbit.
And if they're quite posh, and wear Harris Tweed,
In one of their pockets, you'll find carrot seed.

When working in winter, with solder and fittings,
In a plumber's pockets, are warm woollen mittens.
When buying his equipment, he's given a docket.
And guess where he puts it, straight into his pocket.

When you start work and a tradesman become,
You'll need special trousers, so go tell your mum.
If your taste in clothes, friends try to mock it.
They're jealous of your trousers, with more than one pocket.

My Long Working Life

Some people are lucky, in their vocation in life,
Getting the wrong job's like getting the wrong wife.
Nine hours a day, dragging around a tool bag.
Then going home to a nagging wife is also a drag.

Nine hours a day, five days a week,
Hating every minute, and your future is bleak.
Fifty years of graft, and nothing good to mention,
Feeling your age, and a pittance of a pension.

Where did it all go wrong, you often stop to think,
Fifty years down a coal mine or at the kitchen sink.
Please let it be over, when will it all end?
Hating your job is like being without a friend.

But some good can come in everyone's life,
Like the company of good friends, children, husband or wife.
Make best of the evenings, weekends and holidays too,
Let retirement change your lifestyle and bring joy to you.

Learn to knit, crochet, or paint, or make a garden seat,
Walk in the country, with friends is something you can't beat.
And join them in the pub, for pie and peas now and then.
And then home to take your tablets, and Horlicks, and in bed by ten.

A Church Secretary's Break

August is here and it's time for a rest,
I've worked hard all year, and I've done our best.
No more activities or meetings, craftwork and such,
I can do our own thing now, thank you very much.

Maybe a holiday in the country, or days by the sea,
No more early mornings, or agendas for me.
A walk in the woods, with friends, on a warm summer's day,
This is life at its best and nothing to pay

Or catching up with the housework, or decorating chores,
Or working in the garden, with midge bites and sores.
But it's a change from the routine; we have all year long,
Its sausages on the barbeque, and singing a song.

A glass of real ale, on a warm summer's night,
Flowers and fruit in the garden, O what a sight.
Good news to all, for Augusts' here once again,
But don't get your hopes up, it's starting to rain.

<u>Ken the Viking</u>

Viking Ken tall and hearty,
Liked nothing better, than a party.
He only had, one constant fear,
Where to get, the perfect beer.

He'd got no barley, hops or oats,
His only hope lay, in his father's boats,.
So he sailed one day, at the crack of dawn.
And sailed into some, far distant morn.

He landed in Ireland, in a bleak summer's fog,
And found a brewery, near an ancient peat bog.
Its ales were dark, and strong and sweet,
And blew the socks, right off his feet.

It's not for me, these dark Irish Ales.
I'll cross the sea tomorrow, and go into Wales.
He entered his boat, feeling quite ill,
And at half past three, he landed in Rhyl.

There's only one cure, he said looking quite pale,
It's a flagon of the finest, strong Welsh light ale.
In Bronwyn's ale house, much to his delight,
He drank the amber nectar, far into the night.

In his search for the best, this drink was quite near,
But alas even this, was not his one perfect beer.
He left Wales that day, and on his face was a frown.
And ended his journey, in fair Rotherham town.

He entered a tavern saying "can I get a meal here",
You certainly can sir, said owner the fair Celia.
During his meal, romance was soon budding,
Partly because, of her grand Yorkshire pudding.

She suggested a drink, like any good landlady oughta,
And at the very first sip, it made his mouth water.
I've ended my search, he said, with a cheer,
I've found me a wife, who brews the perfect beer.

You may think this is rubbish, but believe me it's true,
And if you just listen now, I'll prove it to you.
Centuries have passed, since that search for real ale,
And I'm nearing the end, of my Viking Ken tale.

History repeats itself, I've heard now and then,
For his Viking's ancestors, are also called Celia and Ken.
What a coincidence, this is, you cannot beat that.
And in senior moments, Ken wears a horned hat.

Hats of all Shapes and Sizes

So here' a bit of history, for all that it is worth,
Our ancestors all wore caps, up here in the north.
They wore flat caps like huge dustbin lids
They were once the height of fashion with men and their kids

The fifties kids wore cowboy hats, and Davy Crocket hats to boot,
And pretend to be Hopalong Cassidy, and with cap guns did shoot.
Only grownups then wore proper hats, but their kids they never would,
They'd rather play in the local woods and live like Robin Hood

At the age of eleven, I wore a school cap, but only for one day,
And on my way home from school, I threw that cap away.
With my short trousers, and blazer, I looked a pretty sight,
But wear a cap with a neb on, to me just didn't seem right.

Balaclavas were all the rage, with the kids down our street,
They kept you warm in winter, in frost, snow or sleet.
In the seventies and eighties, caps went out of fashion,
I had a red bobble hat, knitted for me, which I hated with a passion.

Baseball caps were popular, in the north, just a few years ago,
And all the kids wore them, come sun, rain or snow.
I disliked them wholeheartedly, and that's speaking blunt,
Baseball caps were fine with me, but they wore them back to front.

Fleece hats are now all the rage, and I've got a few of these,
They protect your head all day long, against the winter breeze.
You can get gloves, and scarf to match, which to me is sound,
You can buy them in almost any shop, for just about five pound.

I wear mine in the garage, and it really is a must,
It keeps my head as warm as toast, and protects it from saw dust.
Caps were always worn in the north, though southerners may frown,
We've never been keen on bowler hats, as men from London Town.

The Byrley Road Merry Men
(Pronounced Burly Road)
Byrley Road is on Kimberworth Park Rotherham

The Byrley Road merry men,
Were out and about, by half past ten.
Down Kimi Park Road, in bright procession,
With bow and arrow, our proud possession.
Sometimes we'd walk, and sometimes we ran,
So I'll tell you now, how it all began.

It was one of those life changing events.
That moment when your life changes for the good.
Mine happened in nineteen fifty six,
After watching, the first episode of Robin Hood.

Now Errol Flynn were great, and Richard Todd were good,
But to me and me mates,
Richard Greene, were the real Robin Hood.
He could shoot, an arrow straight and true,
In greenwood, with a bow, made of good English yew.

We watched him throughout the winter,
And archery was now in our blood.
And when summer holidays came at last,
We were straight into Scholes wood.

Woods were just on the doorstep,
And like all other kids under ten.
The first thing we did in Scholes coppice,
Was to make ourselves a new den.

There was plenty of wood to make bows
And arrows, with corn flake box flights.
We'd chase around woods all day,
Fighting for poor people's rights.

We'd choose a big tree for a target,
And practice all day long.
You could stay out till it were dark in the fifties,
Without doing anything wrong.

Life was fun in those days.
In summers, when it never rained.
And health and safety, hadn't been invented,
In a life before blame and claim.

Mum and dad never saw us,
From early morning till night.
From Scholes, to Wentworth and Elsecar,
Our summers were happy and bright.

I still have a yearning to fire arrows,
And I still have a go now and then.
But the happiest days, were in Scholes coppice,
With me mates, me bow and me den.

For we were, the Byrley Road merry men.
Ron, Ron, Les, Dave, Barry, Dennis, Glenn and Ken

Writing Letters

Writing letters is a skill that is disappearing, as each year ends.
We were brought up to write letters, to family and to friends.
We'd get a brand new writing pad, the best that we could buy,
We'd use our favourite fountain pen, in days long gone by.
But the ballpoint became more popular, and it's still the same today,
With pen and paper ready, we'd think of what to say.

In our best hand writing, we'd write dear Malcolm, Jane of friend,
And write our letter neatly, with yours sincerely at the end.
I usually had more than one attempt, before the final draft,
If you read what I had put, you surely would have laughed.
At last our letter was complete, with envelope and stamp,
We'd write the rest another day, for fear of writer's cramp.

I can't remember the last time, I wrote a proper letter,
I stopped doing these years ago, just as I was getting better.
So how do we keep in contact, with friends and family?
My brother uses Facebook, but Email that's for me.
Many people use texts today, those modern day trend setters,
I think I'll fill my fountain pen and write some proper letters.

My Brilliant Friend Ken

If you want to know who wrote that book,
Or the name of that famous TV cook.
If you're unsure of how to spell a word,
Or need the name of that unknown bird.
If you want the recipe for a Christmas cake,
Or need to know which pill to take.
For all these things, and so much more,
It just takes a knock, on my neighbour's door.

If you need to know how to fix a tap,
Or on a ceiling how to fill that gap.
At household chores, he knows what he's at,
He makes beans on toast and Hoovers the mat.
Is there anything he doesn't know?
Compared to him, all the others are slow.
He can even wire a plug, and build a shed,
He's even wise when asleep in bed.

**Trust me
I'm a GENIUS**

If you can't remember how to dance,
Or know the capitals of Spain or France.
What is the name of that lively tune?
Or the maker of that that silver spoon.
Who won that race in eighty seven?
Or the quickest way to get to Devon.
For all these things and so much more,
It just takes a knock on my neighbour's door.

His wife and daughter just dote on him,
As do his niece, and brother in law Jim.
His good friend Ron, when things he needs to know,
Always knows just where to go,
This wise man's wife admits to all who call,
That her husband is a know it all.
So if you want to know, who, or why, or what, or when,
Just knock on his door and ask for Ken.

The Fashion King of Kimberworth Park

I have always been a fashion King,
And always bought the latest thing.
I was proud to wear my yellow cords.
My orange shirt was cool beyond words.
I always thought that my clothes were great,
That a keen sense of fashion was my fate.
I was dressed to kill as a single gent,
With Rupert trousers wider than a tent.

I have always had a great fashion sense,
With none of your shirts for fifty pence,
Shirts with lace frills, in nineteen sixty eight,
At twenty one, I thought I looked great,
My wardrobe was packed with stunning arrays,
Of kipper ties and flares, from happier days.
I'd go out for a drink, on a Saturday night.
All decked out in the latest black and white.

Idyllic days of fashion, in my youthful days.
When Tootal ties, were the latest craze.
With my checked sports Jacket, and winkle picker shoes,
I was every girl's dream, so how could I lose,
I was a fashion king, and thought I looked grand,
But something was wrong, but I didn't understand.
What I learned in later years, I really should have known,
A wife picks a man's clothes, as well as her own.

No more narrow checked trousers and loud pink shirts,
To throw out my treasured clothes, now that really hurts.
I'd only been married, barely one week and a day,
When out went my Rupert's, what a colourful array
My orange shirt, and my yellow cords went next,
I have to admit I was so extremely vexed.
Even my bright lime green trunks, in which I went swimming,
In fact all of my clothes, that were so attractive to women.

Ronald Town

What can I say, with all my confidence gone?
I'm not like that far away vision, of fashion king Ron,
My last three suits have been chosen by women,
And I've nothing to wear, with which to go swimming.
Once I was known as top of the pops,
Now all my clothes come from charity shops.
I'm older now; I don't worry these days, and try to keep calm,
I now wear clothes for comfort, and clothes that are warm.

Ron's Bad Hair Day

There's none in this group has anything to say,
About what it means to have a real bad hair day.
I lost my hair on a summer's afternoon,
At nineteen years old, in the middle of June.
When you hear about it now, you can have a good laugh.
How I lost my hair, whilst having a bath.

I soaked in the bath for over an hour,
The reason for this is that you can't read in the shower.
I'd read all my Sci-Fi about Martians and space ships,
And dream about supper and a nice plate of fish and chips.
Looking back now, reminds me that life's really not fair,
For when I emptied the bath, it was full of my hair.

The very next morning, whilst fitting a hinge,
My mates were appearing, to look at my fringe.
It was two inch further back, than it had been the day before,
It still lay in the bath, and not on the barber's shop floor.
How could a teenager go to the pub, or a dance at the Carlton,
With a haircut that resembled, the great Bobby Charlton.

Over the years I've faced ridicule and sneers,
From family and friends, and some of my peers.
But now things have changed, at the coming of a new age.
For haircuts like mine, are now all the rage.
With my brothers, and friends, I can have the last laugh,
They all have less hair than me, as I read in my bath.

A Fight with a Bear

Barry the boxer with his mates at the fair,
Barry the boxer had a fight with a bear.
The bear was in chains, in the ring with his promoter,
A man called Flash Harry, with a new red ford motor.
Harry was a man with plenty to say,
Who's brave enough to fight Bruno, for a ten pound note today.

When Barry stepped forward, his mates thought he'd gone funny,
But Barry was skint, and needed the money.
He'd boxed many men, and knocked them all out,
And as Barry stepped forward, the crowds started to shout.
We'll come to your funeral, and we'll invite the Mayor.
You've no chance at all, in fighting that bear.

Now Barry had a secret, known by just a select few,
His parent had been keepers, in a far off country zoo.
With his sisters and brothers, he'd fed the animals there,
But his particular favourite, had been one Bruno the bear.
When he steeped in that ring, Bruno recognised his friend,
And that wise old bear, knew how to pretend.

It was just a game, they had played long ago.
And they both decided, to put on a show.
Barry quickly went down, with a clunk and a smack,
But soon dear Bruno, lay flat on his back.
Get up said Flash Harry, you're much bigger by far,
If you lose me this fight, I'll have to flog my house and my car.

But shamed and defeated, Flash Harry ran away,
Leaving angry crowds, with unpaid bets that day.
The future for Barry and Bruno, was rosy and fine.
Repeating their act nightly was a little gold mine.
Barry made millions, at the Rotherham Town Fair,
All through the friendship, between Barry, and Bruno the bear.

A Window in Time

The window was invented in 5000 BC,
By an unknown English man, by the name of Billy Bree.
Billy was the first inventor, to live upon this earth.
His parents had chosen Yorkshire, as the place of Billy's birth.
To live in sunny Rotherham, had been his father's dream,
So his son could play for Yorkshire's, famous rock throwing team.

But his father's dreams were shattered, by Billy's attitude,
Billy had been brought up proper and never known to be rude.
I'd rather live in Barnsley, than play that rock throwing game,
I'd even live in Chesterfield, and invent a window frame.
That was too much for his father, that proud Yorkshire man,
If you stay and invent in Rotherham me lad, I'll help you all I can.

So in a cave they named the Domino, they both set up shop,
And invented many useful things, until darkness bade them stop.
Those short dark days in the winter, their livelihood did hinder,
So Billy said to his father we'd better invent that window.
It will give us extra hours of light, if we place a window higher,
And if we want to work after dark, we must also invent some fire.

Using sharpened flint as tools, was not an easy game.
But with much perseverance, they made that first window frame.
Fame came quite quickly, to that creative father and his son,
They became very wealthy, for every cave soon wanted one.
They lived in a close community, and were never alone,
Money had not been invented, so they were paid in lumps of stone.

Rocks and stones were scattered, causing many trips and falls,
Until Billy and his father, invented dry stone walls.
They built them around the village, and laid stones on the road,
But Father had a brainwave "we'll build a stone abode"
But Billy was the brainy one and he always had plenty of nous,
Stone abode sounds silly dad, so let's call this place a house.

Building walls perfected, it soon became their game,
And into each new house they included, a door and window frame.
They built hundreds of new houses, and the years soon came to pass,
Those window frames improved in time, when Billy invented glass.
They built the Domino as their very first pub, and found it quite a lark,
In those happy far off peaceful days, in the stone age Kimberworth Park.

Bread and Jam

In the middle of a wood there lives a man,
Whose only love is bread and jam.
When he was a baby his mother tried,
To change his diet but he only cried.
She tempted him with all things fried,
But he choked on a sausage and nearly died.
A bottle he had whilst in his pram,
Until he discovered bread and jam.

When at Redscope school his teacher said,
You'll not grow strong on jam and bread,
You need some meat and potatoes too,
Apple pies and good beef stew.
The dinner lady, Elsie Fipps,
Tempted him with fish and chips.
Fried pork chops, and eggs and ham,
But the lad held out for bread and jam.

His poor old dad tried a different route
And tempted him with lots of fruit.
Apples and pears and a nice big plum.
But dad gave up trying and sent for his mum.
Who sent him for a psychological test,
While both she and her husband had a rest
They tried to wean him from bread, jam, and butter,
But there was nothing they could do to help this nutter.

On leaving school this teenage nut,
Went to work at Pizza Hut.
At a local store in Rotherham,
He was banned from eating bread and jam.
Pizzas were the company rule,
And bread and jam was not seen as cool.
And Sam as this young man was known,
Went down to only seven stone.

He left this job as soon as he could,
And went to live in Redscope wood.
He made a living by painting scenes,
Of the local church on St. John's green.
Of the Haynook and the Domino pub,
And with the money he bought his grub.
Was it chips or was it ham?
Not on your nelly it was bread and jam.

He's still hidden away and rarely seen,
But can still be found if you're patient and keen.
On summer evenings, just before it gets dark,
If you happen to be passing through Barkers Park.
If the weather is fine, and ne'er a cloud,
Go into the woods and shout out loud,
Are you there, or hey up Sam
And you might just be offered, some bread and Jam.

Celia's Buns

I've never been on a river cruise,
Studied Latin or been on the news.
I've never been on those Great North Runs,
But I've eaten many of Celia's buns,

I've never cycled to Timbuktu,
Sailed on a yacht as one of the crew.
Never skated all day on frozen lakes,
But I've eaten my share of Celia's cakes.

I've never yodelled at dawn from a mountain top
Drunk two gallon of Ben Shaw's fizzy pop
Never admired a gorilla's eyes
But I've eaten dozens of Celia's mince pies

Eating Celia's Pastry is like a dream come true,
It can be eaten with custard, and strawberry ice cream too.
To see husband Ken in action, is quite a surprise.
Eating a plateful of Celia's fruit pies.

Coming Home from School

Coming home from school on washday, on Mondays in my youth,
Was a horrible experience, if I were to tell the truth.
Steam filled all the kitchen, and wet clothes everywhere,
My mother up to her eyes in soap suds was more than I could bear.

Hard work for my mother, as she struggled all year through,
To provide us with our clean clothes, with never a thank you,
Washing, ironing, cleaning, cooking, was sadly hers to do.
Before washers were invented, electric irons and cookers too.

Coming home for lunch on washday, was certainly not cool,
But poor mum was trapped at home, when I went back to school.
I remember mum with fondness, for all she did for us,
A lady from that generation, who did not make a fuss.

I look back upon it all in hindsight, how I often led her a merry dance.
There were many things that she'd have liked to do, but never got the chance.
If only I could turn the clock back, and help her with some chore,
Oh to be coming home for one last time, to see my mum once more.

Ronald Town

Coming Home from Italy

We've scrimped and saved all year long, to go on holiday,
We've read all the brochures, and we've found a place to stay.
Our excitement builds, as the special day draws near,
We're looking forward to our posh hotel, to the sun,
Fine foods and a cool glass of beer.

Our tour guide Sally is the best, and together with our driver Lawrence,
Take us to see Lake Garda, on to Pisa and then to Florence.
We never want to leave this place, with the weather dry and sunny,
We'd carry on all year long, if we only had the money.

They say all good things come to an end, even wine, women and song,
Of course my wife disagrees with me, says it's not where I belong.
We've seen Italy's many wonders from Pompeii, to Sienna and Rome,
But after fourteen days of coach and plane, at last we're coming home.

The Ballad of Ricky Clay

As I walked along the sea shore, upon a summers day.
I happened upon a wise old man, whose name was Ricky Clay.
Ricky was a strange old man, and his clothes were far from new,
His suit was bright yellow, and he only wore one shoe.

He spoke with a Yorkshire accent, and often said e by gum,
I warmed to him quite quickly, for he sounded like my mum.
He was full of wise sayings, like if you meet wild dogs don't bother-em,
With such wisdom that he possessed, I knew he came from Rotherham.

Ricky Clay from down our way, is only sixty three,
His hair is like a bale of hay, and muscles like a tree.
Depending how you treat him, he will either love or hate yer
His wisdom comes from studying, the whole of human nature.

He comes back to Rotherham, once a month each year,
He visits local chip shops and samples local beer.
He visits Kimberworth library to meet the reader's group
He tells them of his travels and how to make oak leaf soup

He goes about the countryside, imparting of his knowledge,
He never went to proper school, he never went to college.
But people seek him out, for his advice, even to this day,
That wise and yellow suited, one shoe man, the legendary Ricky Clay.

Celia's drawer Lament

There are thirty eight drawers in our house and that I find fantastic.
Two of metal, fourteen of wood and the rest are made of plastic.
Drawers are special things, to cherish throughout your life.
And should be shared equally, between a husband and his wife.

Ken made a splendid chest, with twelve drawers made of wood,
And filled eleven drawers with his possessions, as only Kenneth could.
The unfairness of this action, beggar's belief, but it is a fact of life,
He only allocated one small drawer, to Celia his neglected wife.

But this tale has an unhappy ending, which simply was a disgrace,
For in Celia's one and only drawer, she discovered Ken's glasses case.
This caused an upset for that poor lady of proportions off the scale,
So in retaliation, she went on Amazon, and put his scroll saw up for sale.

Ken was distraught and bewildered, at what his wife had done,
So he did what he'd always done, and consulted his friend Ron.
Now Ron was wise and resourceful, and well known for his tact,
But for once he surprised his friend Ken, for it was Celia that he backed.

They discussed the subject all that night, and through the following day,
When you treat your wife unfairly, said our Ron, you often have to pay,
You promised her your worldly goods, so she has what once was yours,
So if you want a quiet life, Kenneth me lad, keep out of Celia's drawers

Flowers I have eaten

Most people have gardens full of flowers, because they look so sweet,
But the flowers in my garden are only there to eat.
I've studied them in detail, and know every component part,
Even Albert Einstein, wouldn't know where to start.
I don't need supermarkets any more, or shop in them for hours,
All my carbohydrates and proteins are provided by my flowers.
You may think that I am crazy, and even start to laugh,
For I even grow geraniums, in my mother's old tin bath.

I supplement my flowers with fruit and veg, and get my five a day,
And I benefit from all this food and never have to pay.
Flowers are my favourite plant, and I've eaten quite a few.
I put poppies in Lasagne, and cowslips in my stew.
I mix daisies with my carrots, and add lupins to my mash,
If you are tempted by my recipes, then why not have a bash.
For lunch on Sunday afternoon, my Yorkshire pud I cook,
With juice extracted from an eggplant, as in my special book.

I have a balanced diet, of fruit, veg, and flowers,
I experiment with plants each day, and while away the hours.
For supper I eat begonias, and cabbage leaves I fry,
For pudding I have rose hip wine, with potato and bluebell pie.
My meals are full of colour, like my famous rainbow flan,
I make it out of clematis flowers, in multi coloured pan.
My neighbours think I'm a hippy, because of my multi coloured life,
Well if they think I'm weird, they should come and meet my wife.

One thing I have failed to do, and I admit to my mistake,
I never have succeeded to bake a wallflower, and a sweet pea cake.
Some foods are not always available, and that's for an obvious reason,
Flowers such a daffodils and bluebells, are restricted to one season.
As I have already stated, the neighbours think I'm a multi coloured hippy,
But I often go incognito, when I sneak to the local chippy,
Each day I keep fit and healthy, and as I run about the room,
My legs are now covered in rose petals, and my ears have begun to bloom.

Jim the woodsman

Down a country lane there walked, a man all dressed in black and green,
He was the finest woodsman that this country's ever seen.
He could fell a tree in half an hour, with a saw and axe so bright,
But he much preferred to fell a tree, by using dynamite.
He was famous for his hand made stools, made from good old English oak.
He sold them for seven and sixpence, to local peasant folk.

His name was Jim the forester, and his lovely wife called Mel,
Who sang in a choir in their domain, and did so very well.
He did gardening for the old folk, in bonny Rotherham Town,
He'd work all day for two and six or in the evening for half a crown.
He'd save shiny florins in a barrel, and when the cask was full.
He'd buy a brand new wagon, his donkey for to pull.
Our Jim was a fitness freak and also quite a menace,
He'd tell jokes to an audience whilst playing table tennis.
In the morning he'd visit a gymnasium, which was named after him,
He'd then run back home again, and was known as speedy Jim.
Once a week he'd visit a local hostelry, come sun or snow or hail,
To eat Yorkshire puddings and sausages and a drink a pint of Theakston's ale

Jim was a gangly outdoors man as handsome as he was tall.
He often walked with a group of friends and invented 'Spot the Ball'.
They walked each week on a Wednesday morn and were a merry band,
And when in the fields they crossed a stile, Jim gave the girls a hand.
They were the finest walkers, this land has ever seen.
Led by local walk leaders and a man dressed in black and green.

The Joys of Decorating

Decorating is such a delight,
Painting doors from morning till night.
Undercoat on and then the gloss,
Working all day long to please the boss.

Stripping walls, will that suit her?
I'd rather play on my computer
Mix the paste and stick the paper,
Love it all, what a caper.

Painting and papering are all done,
Now is the time to have some fun.
But now I have that funny feeling,
That I forgot to paint the kitchen ceiling.

Choosing the colour, not on your life,
My choice comes third after my daughter and wife.
It doesn't match the curtains or suite.
How can a simple man ever compete?

Decorating is such a delight,
Hurrah it's finally Saturday night.
No painting on Sunday she's left in the lurch,
No painting to do when I'm at the church.

My friend Ken likes decorating too,
We both tell our wives there's no more to do.
We've approached our tasks with the upmost of feeling,
You're not done yet, there's that crack in the ceiling

We get out the filler and putty knives too,
We're really uncertain what we have to do.
We apply the caulking from our mastic gun,
Filling gaps in ceilings is so much fun.

Ronald Town

My magic train spotter's hat

I put a hat upon my head and I vanished out of sight,
It was a magic hat you see, and I wore it every night.
You may think I was invisible, but that was not the case,
The hat had just transported me, to a very different place.

I found that hat in Rotherham Town, in a Heart Foundation shop,
It was amongst many other hats, on a shelf right at the top.
It had been there for many years, so one pound I did pay,
It never worked for other folk, for they wore it during the day.

The hat did not endear itself, to people in that shop,
It was pink with yellow and white spots on, with a train stuck on the top.
But when I looked upon that hat, something caught my eye,
It had a magic spell on it, so that hat I had to buy.

Why hadn't it been bought before, is a question you may ask,
It came as a part of a set you see, with an anorak and a flask.
It had belonged to a magic train spotter, a cross eyed man called Bruce,
And could only be sold to a fellow spotter, and one the hat did choose.

The secret of this magic hat, I will try to explain to you,
I put this hat on late at night, and appeared in nineteen sixty two.
I appeared in very bright sunlight, on a platform on a railway station,
It was a different platform every night, much to my elation.

I had a note book with my numbers in, and every name had written,
After many months of spotting, I had visited every place in Britain.
I was the envy of train buffs everywhere, and my fame will never fade,
For after twelve months of spotting, I had seen every loco ever made.

My friends today wouldn't believe me, though I've only got a few.
For the only place that I can prove it, is in nineteen sixty two.
I still go there quite often, though nobody ever knows,
I don't go to spot trains any more, but go to buy very cheap sixties clothes.

How do I get back home, is something you may ask,
I have to take my anorak off, and drink the contents of my flask.
I may dispose of my hat one day, and my adventures then will stop.
Then you too can buy my hat, at the Heart Foundation shop.

My Working Life

Work for some people is a joy to behold,
For others it's a lifetime of doing what you're told.
Doing a job which you love is full of joy and thrills.
But for most people it's a means, of paying all the bills.

In my early working life, I enjoyed working with wood,
And drew intense pleasure, when creating something good.
Cutting dovetails and tenons, making cupboards and doors
Enjoying making things, that other considered chores.

The affinity with tools and hardwood, is a lifetime affair,
Carving exotic pew ends, or making a dog leg stair.
Sharp steel on wood, is a craftsman's delight,
When working from early morning, and far into the night.

But the time comes when priorities change, and the joy seems to fade.
Supporting a family then comes first, and bills need to be paid.
You still do your work, and gain pleasure by a job well done.
But the joy of long hours creating, no longer seems to be much fun.

But in the third stage in life, if you only admit the truth,
You work again for pleasure, and regain something of your youth.
Old skills are recaptured, by working with your hands once again.
Retirement is a pleasure, if you can put up with the pain.

My dream Holiday

My dream Holiday would have to be,
A tour of the world for my wife and me.
To see the seven wonders, or those that still remain,
And travel through the continents, on a famous steam train.

If I was long haired, and a young man once again.
I'd pose on the beaches, in far off sunny Spain.
But now I'm short of hair, and almost far too old,
I go each year on holiday, and drive to where I am told.

There are a number of places, that I would like to see,
If I was a young man again, both rich and fancy free.
I'd visit the pyramids of Egypt, and see the mighty sphinx.
Much better than washing dishes, stood at kitchen sinks.

To see once again works of art, in Florence's fair city,
And appear to all the ladies, as someone who's quite witty.
Or live on a coral island, surrounded by warm seas.
And live on the produce, from luxurious tropical trees.

Or visit ancient ruins, in far off distant lands,
Or dig for pirate's treasure, on warm golden sands.
An archaeologist on television, I would long to be,
And travel the world over, with the good old BBC.

I'd fly to New Zealand, on a plane with very large wings,
To see where they filmed the Hobbit, and Lord of the Rings.
But to be entirely honest I've only saved a few quid,
So I'll have to be content this year, with a holiday in Brid.

Who is the very first?

An historian or archaeologist, is what I'd choose to be,
I think about it every day, from noon till half past three.
I'd specialise in discovering, who was the very first,
This would be a difficult task, but I'd try until I burst.
Who was the first to discover fire, or build a wall of stone,
I'd find the very first caveman's axe, and keep it for my own,.

I'd study from the age of ten, and read many books and think,
Who was the very first person, to write with pen and ink?
I'd meet many famous people, wearing polished shoes or wellies,
Some of them would be on Time Team that we see on our telly's
I'd dig for Roman artefacts in Britain, Italy and Bahrain,
I'd find the first minted coin, and the first woodworker's plane.

I'd write the history of first things, and be as happy as can be,
When I discover the first person, who first chopped down a cedar tree.
The first person to use a spanner, and fly and airplane.
And who first discovered seams of coal, and who used it on a train
I'd learn who first made trousers, to cover up their knees,
Was the person who invented the needle and thread, a lady called Denise?

I'd dig in ancient Egypt, and discover Pharaoh's tombs,
And discover gold and silver, in subterranean rooms.
Who first made wheels with spokes in, I'd discover in that place,
And discover Cleopatra's wedding dress, made linen and of lace.
I'd read all the famous cookery books, and discover if I could,
The person who became famous, by making Yorkshire pud.

I'd discover who invented fish and chips, and made tomato sauce,
Or who was the first jockey, to ride upon a horse.
Who invented porcelain, and made the first dinner plate.
Or the very first carpenter, to make a garden gate.
I'd have the time of my life, discovering who made things first,
Like who made the first barrel of beer, to quench their ancient thirst.

I'd find the first painting, in some unknown British cave,
And if I'm lucky I'll also discover, the very first man to have a shave.
I'd have loved to live this enchanted life, of strawberries and cream,
But I know that it's too late now, and it is just a dream.
But my life so far I don't regret, and this will make amends,
I wouldn't miss one moment now, among my dearest friends.

The Yorkshire Time Traveller

Fred the Yorkshire time traveler visited the universe in a shed.
His first visit was to a world where skies were all bright red
He then visited a world where the trees were only just budding,
Then came back to Rotherham, for his mother's Yorkshire pudding.
He was born in the thirteenth century the son of country squire,
He trained in the use of weapons and arrows he did fire.

He'd lived many years and had seen many sights,
He lived during the war of the roses, and had been in many fights.
During one tiring battle, as he longed for his bed,
A hillside just exploded, revealing a weird looking shed.
Fred approached the shed carefully with a certain amount of dread
Not realising that this wooden hut was a time traveller's shed.

To open that shed door, our Fred he tried his hardest,
When landing beside him suddenly was Dr Who's TARDIS.
You've discovered a lost time machine said the Doctor to our Fred
But first let's get away from this battle, before we both end up dead.
They entered the police box together and accompanied by a strange sound,
And materialized inside the new time machine that our Fred had just found.

By the authority of a Time Lord, Doctor Who said,
You are now an honorary Time Lord, and I'm giving you this shed.
To travel through time and space, doing good to all types of creatures,
But before I leave you I'll explain, your time machine's best features.
The chameleon circuit is broken; that means it's kaput and its dead,
For the rest of your life it will always be, disguised as a garden shed.

The Doctor explained how to work this new shed,
It's a series fifty time machine which meant nowt to our Fred.
You can go where you like, be you happy or be you glum,
But once every year back to Yorkshire you certainly must come,
The secret of a Time Lord's long life, I can now to you reveal,
Is eating Yorkshire Pudding, at the annual Christmas meal.

Worst ever Christmas presents

At Christmastime long ago, when I was almost six,
I badly wanted a big red car, but I got some wooden bricks.
I wrote to Father Christmas, and put in a complaint,
We've no cars left replied Santa, and so he sent a tin of paint.
It's the same colour as my bedroom door, I told my mum that day,
That Santa doesn't miss a trick, was all she had to say.

When I was eight, I was asked what I would like,
I answered immediately, and said, it's got to be a bike,
A bike's too dear said mother, you'll have to think again.
The bike went up the spout that day, and I got a clock work train.
I was happy to get a train, that was painted green and black,
But when it came it was no use, for they couldn't afford the track.

I wanted a painting set about the age of ten,
With watercolours and brushes, and a permanent black pen.
But instead I got box of games, and a pair of shoes that were too bright,
I hated games with a passion, and the shoes they were too tight,
When I complained to mum and dad, they sent me straight to bed.
Why ask me what I really want, when no one listens to what I said.

At fourteen I asked for a tool set, from the club book we had at home,
Please don't let me down, this time dad, and buy me a garden gnome.
Or buy me clothes that I don't like, a record or a pair of football boots,
Or a Roy Rogers cowboy outfit, with a gun that never shoots.
But to my surprise I got my tools, and didn't feel so daft.
But I started my job as a joiner that year, and mum and dad both laughed.

Once at work the presents stopped, and this was a relief to me,
No more useless presents, I've had since the age of three.
I've never been jealous of my two brothers; I'd never go that far,
But the very year I started work, my brother got a big bright red car.
My other brother also was asked, what he would really like,
And to my surprise he got that year, a brand new two wheel bike.

My wife's won the lottery

It was one morning in June that changed my life,
It began with scream from darling wife.
I've won five million pounds, was all she could say,
I put two quid on the lottery, just the other day.
Now this was a shock, the biggest one so far,
I can have a big house now, and a shining new car.

I could drive my red Ferrari in Italy and Spain,
And when I come back home, I would buy a big steam train.
I'd buy a cottage in Scarborough, and all my friends I'd invite,
It would have fifteen large bedrooms, all painted apple white.
The things we could do with five million in cash,
I've never been sailing, but I can now have a bash.

Now don't get too excited, just try and stay calm,
I'm spending my lottery winnings, on a nice big country farm.
We've got to plan our future, and not waste all this cash,
I can't talk to you now my dear, to the bank I must dash.
She knows what she's doing, no need for alarm.
But do I want to really live, in a smelly old country farm.

The things I could do with half of that money,
I'd help my family and friends, and my days would be sunny.
Wait till she comes back home, I will try and makes her see sense.
I don't want to spend my days spreading manure, or mending a broken fence
She came back all excited, and this started all the rows,
She'd spent all the money on a farm, and a herd of two hundred cows

What about my new cars, and holidays in the sun,
Milking cows at dawn, is not my idea of fun.
Planting crops in the spring, I just aint gonna do,
And the best place for animals is in London zoo.
The money had all gone now, and so I started to scream,
Then I woke up in bed, to find it was only a dream.

The Eternal Optimist

I hope I'm not late for work again it is a fear of mine
My train was due at eight O'clock and now it's ten past nine.
I am an eternal optimist my glass is always half full.
But I hope my train takes me to Brid, and not to blinking Hull

I hope my boss will understand, if I am late once again
I run courses in positive thinking so I hope I catch my train.
I am an eternal optimist my glass is always half full.
But although my job pays really well it is a load of bull.

I hope these trousers still fit me, and I don't need a bigger size
Maybe I should change my diet and not live on chips and pies.
I am an eternal optimist my glass is always half full.
But I'll buy trousers with an elastic waist, when I get to Brid or Hull.

I hope I don't fall asleep while travelling on this train.
And when I get to Bridlington, it doesn't start to rain
I am an eternal optimist my glass is always half full.
I've forgotten my umbrellas I always buy in Hull.

I never used to be like this, so worried and uncertain,
I'd never watch a horror film from behind the front room curtain.
I am an eternal optimist my glass is always half full.
But while I've been pondering, I've arrived in blinking Hull.

I've just had a text message from my boss, and my eyes are getting full.
He's given up all hope on me, and transferred my job to Hull.
I am an eternal optimist my glass is always half full.
But I've grown rather fond of Brid and I'm not so sure of Hull.

My Keys are Missing

I'm late for that meeting and I am ill at ease,
I wish I could remember, where I've put my blooming keys.
I ask my darling wife, but of course it is no use,
You'd lose your head, my lad if only it were loose.
Where did you have them last, then she said to me?
If I knew that woman, you know that's where I'd be.

I've looked in my coats and trousers and even in my shoes,
Of all the times and days, for my keys for to lose.
Peter's on the telephone the meetings just begun,
Being a church secretary is certainly not much fun.
Start without me I say, I'll be a quick as I can be,
In desperation I'd better try, down the back of the settee.

Use you spare set my wife cries out,
I've lost them too, and I start to shout.
Lower your voice don't shout at me,
It's not me who's lost their keys.
Not having my keys just now is such a wrench,
Off to the garage once again, to look on the joiner's bench

I empty out the waste bin and cause a stink,
Did you have to do it in the kitchen sink?
I move all the furniture including that heavy chair,
I find 50p and a ginger nut but my keys are not there.
It was then I remembered, just where my keys are,
I left them in the ignition, for I never locked the car.

I get to church quite quickly but the meeting it is over,
To find the vicar is just getting into, her brand new shiny Rover.
Hello there, I'm sorry I'm late the vicar hears me shout,
Don't worry, It'll not happen again Ron, you've just been voted out.
I go home happy and ecstatic, singing and so full of glee,
There'll be no taking notes again, or typing minutes for me.

Cowboy Builders

Jack the bricklayer tall and blonde
Built a house near our local pond.
He built it nearer than he oughta
And put his garage in the water.
Instead of cars that wouldn't float
Inside he kept a rowing boat.

Pete the plumber small and thick
Put in a sink all made of brick.
He built it higher than he should
In the middle of the local wood.
In the sink were many gaps
And nowhere to connect his taps.

Ron the joiner young and merry
Went to work in scarf and beret.
He led his master quite a dance
Looking like a lad from France.
His only tool was a brace and bit
His master told him what to do with it.

Dave the plasterer broad and tall
Spread his plaster on the wall.
To him this was the thing to do
But he spread it with his girlfriend's shoe.
He gave the foreman quite a shock
By making it smooth with his sock.

Maurice the electrician tall and wise
Gave his wife quite a surprise.
By wiring up her freshly baked bread
She thought he'd gone funny in the head.
When cutting a slice it gave her a fright
By switching on the kitchen light.
No more wiring for you, said his poor wife
Grow up lad and get a life.

The Man who never shaves

In a land beneath the waves lives a man who never shaves.
He was born to parents who, lived on fish and never stew.
Fish was dear so they did save, and buy a des res under water cave
People thought that they were weird, because mother and son grew a beard

In a land beneath the waves lives a man who never shaves.
His beard is as long as it can get that once he used it as fishing net.
Cod and herring he has caught, and a dozen squid with ne'er a thought
Dog fish too that never bark, until one day he caught a shark.

It pulled his beard and dragged him far, in that under water tug of war.
From Whitby harbour to Japan, and back to where it first began.
The old man thought he'd had his lot, when the shark got tied up in a knot.
Learn a lesson from this man so brave, and every morning have a shave.

Patron Saint

I heard this story from my dad
On a night that was wet and dark.
He told me that our Patron Saint
Was really born on Kimberworth Park.
He said it was a family secret
Passed down from father to son.
And as I was the one hundredth descendant
I must now tell everyone.
All this happened Long ago
Even before dogs had learned to bark.
When a lad called George was born to a poacher
Who lived on ancient Kimberworth Park.

George learned all the tricks from his father
And with a longbow he became an ace,
He shot deer and rabbits and squirrels,
And caught pheasants by the brace.
He learned to wrestle and fight with his fists
And to fight with sword and spear.
Until he became famous throughout the land
And the king of him did hear.
He sent his emissary to Rotherham
And bid George to come to the royal palace.
George replied, I'll come if I can bring my sheepdog Ben,
And my pretty young wife called Alice.

Now young George had a whale of a time,
With King Edgar and all his mates.
And every evening he would sign autographs,
Outside the palace gates.
King Edgar was very proud of George,
And thought his manner so quaint,
And within six months our canny Yorkshire lad,
Was made England's second Patron Saint.
He went on a state tour of England,
Along with Alice and sheepdog Ben,
And on his return to London,
He lived in Downing Street at number ten.

But back home things were not the same;
Things had gone from bad to worse,
And folk back there on Kimberworth Park
Seemed to be living under a curse.
The cause of all this upset was Ceredig,
a mighty Green Welsh Dragon,
Who had settled on a hilltop near Kimberworth manor
Behind a brewers wagon.
The people rallied round to fight him,
But couldn't do a thing,
And after all else had failed to work,
They pleaded with Edgar their king.

Edgar sent for George that evening,
And told of this tragic news
So George gathered men together,
With bows made from the finest English yews.
With Alice and Ben beside him
He set out for Kimberworth Park.
And to boost the morale of George and his army
Ben his sheepdog had started to bark
He landed back home on a Wednesday
And met up with mum, dad and his mates.
And by early Thursday morning
He was camped by the manor house gates.

Ceredig started to attack them,
And singed the hair of many a man,
Until George invented the helmet,
By using his mother's copper saucepan.
Green Dragon stood defiantly
On top of hill where pub now stands today
The proud English bowmen started firing,
And continued firing arrows all that day.
While George sneaked up behind dragon
And pierced his heart with his broad sword,
He toppled off hill with Ben barking,
But Green Dragon never again said a word.

From that day George was a hero
And celebrated throughout this proud land.
And venison and chips were on the menu,
Jelly and custard and a thirty piece band.
It was the 23rd of April when it happened
Which is now known as St. George's Day
And each year on the eve of that great victory
We eat pie and peas together at Green Dragon
And only four pound to Pay.
No one now remembers where George fought this battle
Or the story of Alice and Ben.
But I sometimes hear a sheepdog barking,
When I visit the Green Dragon pub now and then.

Paper

Paper was invented by the Egyptians in the third century BC,
Made from papyrus or the bark of the fig, mulberry and also the Daphne tree
It revolutionised the world back then, and does the same today
Some paper products are expensive but willingly we pay.
It has so many uses, and it's not as simple as it looks,
It's used for writing letters, and making wallpaper and also reading books.
Without paper creative writing groups, would certainly cease to exist,
With nothing to write our poems on it surely would be missed.

We'd struggle in our painting group if paper was not there
Without paper in our libraries the shelving would be bare.
If we wrote and painted on plywood just think what we'd have to pay
The origami masters from the orient would all be out of work today.
Paper makes life much better and nothing could be finer
And paper that we know today was invented in 1st century China
The Chinese and Japanese use it for their houses, up to the present day
But with the British climate, a paper house, would certainly wash away.

There is a strange rumour, hereabout, that paper was invented near this place
By an ancient Yorkshire lad with woad upon his face
He was the village idiot and his name was Michael Ugman Bevan,
He spent his time carving his name on trees, until he was eleven.
There had to be a better way, than this tree engraving caper,
It was wearing away his finger nails, so he invented tree bark paper.
He boiled mulched up bark in cooking pots, much to his mother's ire,
But the mixture soon dried out, beside the kitchen fire.

The resultant paper soon dissolved, Michael's mothers rage,
It was heralded the greatest thing, and the marvel of the age,.
He made his fame and fortune, and became richer than good king Will,
And he went on to invent pen and ink, which made him richer still.
Now you may think that this is pure fiction, and a bit of a lark,
But from that day you never saw, his name carved on any oak tree bark.
To say that the Chinese invented paper in AD 127
Is an insult to the memory of Michael Ugman Bevan.

Go Carts on Kimberworth Park

Over fifty years I can see it still,
Our home-made go cart speeding down the hill.
This wooden wonder O what a joy,
The proud possession of any boy.
A set of pram wheels was the start,
Of this nineteen fifties sleek go cart.
A pair of wheels nailed to the plank,
Is far better than money in the bank.

An orange box fixed at the rear,
In front, are wheels from which to steer.
A rope attached and then we're ready,
Our new go cart is strong and steady.
Down the hill the risks we take,
Too late now to fit a brake.
We level out come to a stop,
And buy sweets from our local shop.

Chewing sweets what a thrill
Then drag the trolley back up the hill
Out of breath we never learn,
We just can't wait for our next turn,
It's getting late and time for bed,
Our new go cart's in the shed.
A fitting garage for our new toy,
A lovely time to be a young boy.

School Days

When I started school as a little lad it was in days of old
You spoke only when spoken to and did what you were told.
If you broke the rules at school you never did so again
For you often got the slipper, or the dreaded teacher's cane.
I got the cane twice myself, and it certainly left its mark,
I learned a valuable lesson then, of knowing when not to talk.

Apart from the punishment, my Junior School I did enjoy,
I played with my mates at playtime like any normal boy.
I loved history, craft and literature and singing my favourite hymn
Junior school was marvellous, and it was there I learned to swim.
At all sport I was terrible, but I loved to paint and draw,
And making things from balsa wood, with a fine bladed saw.

At eleven I went to secondary school, and walked there with my mates,
But all the laughter and fun ended, as we entered our school gates.
Who made the rules at this new school; I bet that no one knows,
You couldn't run in corridors, or wear your choice of clothes.
The teachers had their favourites, like David, Ian or James,
The rest of us did not exist; we were the ones who hated games.

The lessons that I loved were History, literature, science and art,
I hated geography and sport most of all, and dreaded taking part,
But the highlight of the week for me, was making things with wood,
I'd saw and plane all afternoon, if the teacher said I could.
I wanted to study geology, and make myself a name,
But qualifications I had none, and a joiner I became.

Looking back now in hindsight now, school set me up for life
I learned to love the written word in common with my wife.
The skills I learned in woodwork I remember to this day,
How to sharpen planes and chisels, and saw wood the proper way.
I meet old school mates every week, and our friendship will always last,
 And all the things I didn't like from school, are now faded into the past.

My Sporting Achievements

Why couldn't I play football like many of my mates, I tried to as a lad?
Each year I had a case ball, at Christmas, from my mum and dad.
I'd kick it in a straight line, to a goal at the end of the pitch,
But it would go where I didn't want it to, and end up in a ditch.

Why couldn't I play tennis like Peter, Dave or Mick,
I'd hit the ball into the net, or out of bounds I never learned the trick.
I'd always jump the wrong way, and never return the ball,
I tried all the sports as a lad, and failed at them all.

I wasn't bad at short distance running, but the javelin I liked the most.
Until I just missed the teachers head and pierced out new goal post.
The teacher decided I'd no aptitude, along with my mates Malcolm and Chris,
They sent us to the library every Tuesday, and we'd give PE a miss.

I loved all the lessons, that didn't involve a racket ball or bat,
Woodwork was a favourite, and I became quite good at that.
I loved science and history, and came the top of the class,
But Geography I really hated and hardly got a pass.

English literature was my passion, writing stories I loved best,
And surprisingly I even loved the daily English spelling test.
I couldn't wait for the PE lessons, to which my mates so longed to go,
And I'd go along to the library, and write stories of long ago.

Bungee Jumping

You need to do your daily exercise my physio said to me,
Sitting watching television all day long will aggravate your knee.
Twice a day laid on your back and on your stomach too,
If you want your hamstring to get better it's entirely up to you.
I'm bored with lifting up my leg and all that boring stuff,
So I decided to do a bungee jump and that should be enough.

Of bungee jumping as a sport I've always been a fan,
So I started in a simple way off my neighbour's caravan.
And now my physio gives me an extra workout, to fix my other knee,
Now I limp on two legs, I'm as happy as can be.
When I am cured I'm gonna have, bungee lessons from the very best,
So I asked my friend Marilyn for whom she would suggest.

I found that she was an expert, and in that sport an ace.
She lives in a place called Redcar that north eastern seaside place.
She's often jumps off Morrison's roof and bounces up and down,
She's known as Redcar's answer to Tigger, in famous northern town.
But husband Pete was furious, and with Marilyn did beg,
If those cycle inner tubes come apart, you're bound to break a leg.

So I went to her for lessons, on how to bungee jump,
But my wife Valerie put the spoke in, and gave me such a thump.
Why do you always have stupid hobbies, can't you just read a book.
Or have lessons from Mary berry, and learn how to really cook.
Now I'm sad and embarrassed, for to really tell the truth,
I've told my mates, I'm going to jump, off Marks and Spencer's roof,

The Knocker up of Old Kimberworth Circa 1900

A village near old Rotherham town was as quiet as can be,
The only noise to be heard for miles, were birds up in a tree.
No person stirred on High street, or within that village fair,
Where are all our children, all the school teachers did declare?

At Jenkins boiler works, Sir Robert said, on the stroke of ten,
I've got workers from all over, but where are my Kimberworth men?
The brickyards were half empty, on that fateful Friday morn,
When those lazy men get here, they'll wish they'd never been born.

The winding wheel at the pit was still, for those men were missing too,
And all the men stood idle for there, was nothing they could do.
The local farmer on Kimberworth Park, was in a state of panic too,
His cows needed milking at six O clock, and it was almost half past two.

Beatson Clark was just the same, for no furnace men meant no glass,
For the men who came, what could they do, but sit upon their ass.
Local iron works were depleted, for the canteen staff did not turn up,
The men had a liquid lunch at the local pub, and pale ale they did sup.

The police and military were called, and to Kimberworth they went,
They set up shop near the manor house, in a Khaki coloured tent.
They walked around those quiet streets, to assess the situation,
They said that the silence was the result, of a cunning foreign invasion

At four O clock they heard a noise, as people from their houses came,
They'd let their employers down, and would never live down the shame.
The village called a meeting, to discover who caused this situation,
Ben Roddison was the culprit, and knocking up was his occupation.

Poor Ben hid behind the backs, of son Enoch and Fanny Ben's fair wife,
The crowd were getting angry, and Ben was fearful for his life.
Explain how this happened, said Chief Constable Gilbert Oswald Hale,
And Ben explained to police chief and his neighbours, this sad and sorry tale.

Ben was the local knocker upper, and was a conscientious man,
But the night before in the Traveller's Inn, started drinking black and tan.
After 15 pints Ben and Fanny staggered home, after having so much to sup,
And didn't get up in the morning to wake the village up.

Ronald Town

The moral of this story is, if you want to get up for work each day,
Is to buy a new alarm clock, out of your very next week's pay.
And ban knocker up Ben and wife Fanny, from local pubs during the week,
And once again Ben was seen with pole in hand but of beer he did not reek.

So if you wanted knocking up, back then, Benjamin Roddison was your man,
For he became a reformed character and never again drank black and tan.

David the Blacksmith

David the blacksmith at his forge, in thirteen forty two,
In a hut full of smoke invented, the very first chimney flue.
It was an old bent iron pipe, connected to his furnace,
So proud of his work was David, he showed it to his wife Bernice.
But like all women of a certain argumentative type,
She wasn't at all impressed by David's bent iron pipe.
Said it was too hot; the wrong colour and the wrong size as well,
She harped on this all that week and gave husband David hell.
So David was annoyed, dejected, depressed and ended up feeling sick,
And so the very next day he invented a chimney that was all made of brick.
His wife Bernice was surprised, ecstatic, pleased and started to grovel,
Until David, annoyed and fed up, built her a fire place inside of their hovel.
The moral of this story and a warning to all men in this life,
If you invent something special don't show it to your wife.
David realized that old iron is for scrap men and those men who are thick,
So he packed in his blacksmith work and build chimneys out of brick.

Friends

Loneliness is a fact of life for many in our world today,
As children we have many friends, with whom we love to play.
Some remain friends throughout our lives,
For many of us our special friend is our husbands or our wives.

Loneliness can be overcome, and brought to an end,
All it takes is someone, who cares and wants to be our friend.
Friends are special people, the ones who always care,
The ones who at times when life is hard, you know are always there.

Friends are not perfect people, and don't always get it right.
But friends see beyond our faults and failures, and then our future's bright.
Friends often have shared interests, like creative writing, arts and crafts.
But often it's just being together, for a natter and lots of laughs.

Friendship is contagious and it often starts with one,
And one friend leads to another, and then another one.
Oh loneliness where are you now, that blight that never ends?
I've no time to be lonely now; I'm with my special friends.

I Want to Live Forever

If you could live forever, Imagine what you could see.
See all our future monarchs, and an acorn become a great tree.
If you could live forever and stay as young as a pup.
You could see a Yorkshire man wins at Wimbledon,
Or Rotherham win the FA cup.

If you could live forever, imagine what you could be.
The driver of the first No 39 hover bus
Or be a passenger on a space ship for free.
If you could live forever, imagine what you could be
The first man to reach one thousand, or own a forty foot TV.

If we could all live forever, imagine the things we would see
At our 100th birthday, we'd have another bring and share tea
Imagine if we all live forever, we'd see new steam locos once again
And visit Rotherham Station on a Saturday.
And see the Mallard in steam again

If we could live forever, none of us would have to go far
To see the first female Archbishop,
In Westminster Abbey playing an electric Guitar
The Abbey would have to be extended
I think that it would be rather good news,
To see 10,000 in the congregation
And half of them jumping up and down in the pews.

I want to live forever imagine what I could do
See all my clothes go out of fashion, and that goes for computers too.
I really don't want to live forever, imagine what I would have to do
Make sure all my unfinished jobs were completed.
For my wife has lived forever too.

Transparent Daisy and Invisible Dan

There lived a girl on St. John's Green
Who was always there but never seen.
The reason soon became apparent
Daisy Keyworth was transparent.
Daisy couldn't be seen in late afternoon or at night
But only when the sunshine, was extremely bright.

Her elder brother was a boy named Dan
He was the Kimberworth Park invisible man.
Their condition was the envy of all that they met
Especially Charlie Dowson and his pretty sister Jet.
They met at night and they fell in love
At night in the dark with no moon above.
Dan and Jet were married that year
In St. John's Church by a Reverend so dear.
You may kiss the bride said the vicar behind him
I'll do that with pleasure said Jet, if only I can find him.
I'll find you said invisible Dan on that special happy day
And if vicar can find me the wedding fees I'll pay.

Lock all the doors said the vicar all abash
He's not getting out without paying me the cash.
Now Charlie and Daisy sister of the groom,
We highly embarrassed they soon left the room.
They met in the hall and drank up their coffees
Saying when we get wed it'll be at Registry Office.

If ever at midday you're on St. John's Green
And strange things are happening and no one can be seen.
Get close to the trouble or as close as you can
And I bet you'll hear the voices of Daisy and elder brother Dan.
There's a moral to this story and its meaning is apparent
Keep away from invisible men and girls who are transparent.

In a land called Sunshine

In a land called Sunshine so long ago
Where it didn't rain and it didn't snow.
Living there was a race of tall handsome men
Whose names were all Brian, Ron or Ken.
Those ancient men they all worked like troopers
Some were railway guards or joiners and the rest were coopers.

Their women folk were wild and fierce
And every blond lady was called Denise.
Some helped their men folk making oak barrels
But only the Celias, Elaines and the carols.
In this sunny land they only worked until one
In the afternoons they enjoyed the warm summers sun.

The Denise's were exempt from all work in the city
They just had to sun bathe drink wine and look pretty.
They lived their lives free from trouble and care
And spent every morning combing their hair
They earned no money and these are the facts
They lived off the others who paid income tax.

As numbers continued to grow a problem occurred
A problem so great the like had never been heard.
In a factory built for mass producing oak Barrels
They now employed two hundred and twenty two Carols.
One hundred Celias and fifty seven called Elaine
A problem that even the Ken's could never explain.

It was a problem so great with no one to blame
For every Carol looked exactly the same.
It was the same with Celia, Denise and Elaine
All the girls were pretty and no one was plain.
The men were the same and that was not on.
How can you choose from two hundred men called Ron.

When a name was called out to go and see the boss
Hundreds turned up and he was always so cross.
The easy answer was their names had to change
But no other name was allowed in that land so strange.
It was written in laws from the beginning of time

That seven names only could be used in the land of Sunshine.

Production dropped and it was far from funny
For Ken their new boss lost a shed load of money.
Then Ken grew angry and threatened the sack
When the problem was solved by putting a number on their back.
When a person was called to partake of a brew
The Tannoy called our come in Carol one hundred forty two.

The land called Sunshine was again happy and pleased
And a new industry emerged through an Idea by a Denise.
It was started overnight by a Brian, Elaine and Ron
Who made one off tee shirts with names and numbers on.
Wedding vows also changed to bring an end to all strife
Do you Ken 92 take Celia 27 to be your dearly beloved wife?

Where the Pooch tree grows

In a far off land where the pooch tree grows
Live a tribe of giants with fifteen big toes.
They live off the fruit of this abundant tree
And with its wood made ships that sail on the sea.
The tree grows so tall and can be seen for miles
From Greenland's shores to the Canary Isles.
So useful was this resilient wood
Many came to cut it if only they could.

But the residents of the land were far from barmy
And twenty foot giants form an invincible army.
The loggers gave up and because of their greed
Were sentenced for life the giants to feed.
The trees are still there and it will always be so
For the giants secret weapon was a massive big toe.
So if you visit this land to look at these trees
You'll only come up to the youngest giant's knees.

Show them respect and if you're very good
They'll send you back home with a sample of wood.
But only a sample not a trunk, plank or even some fruit
For the multi toed giants have learned how to shoot.
In a far off land where the pooch tree grows
Live a tribe of giants with fifteen big toes.
Times for them has changed and no one needs their boats.
So they weave bark from the Pooch tree into fine winter coats.

Married Bliss

My friend's house is a place I like to go
To hear the latest news all the things I need to know.
But I often have a problem and a decision which to make
Just whose side in an argument tonight I will have to take.
Then Celia said, you'll never believe what Ken has done today
Is something I'm quite accustomed to and expect to hear her say.

I've had another bad day and feeling out of sorts
And Ken has done nothing to help me I regret I have to report.
I've vacuumed the carpets you can't deny that I've done that,
What! She cried out with a yell, all you've done is the back door mat.
Not knowing what to say I gave her a knowing smile,
It must be the cleanest doormat that I've seen for quite a while.

That's not all he's done she said with emotion and strong feeling,
He decided to fill that crack today in the middle of the ceiling.
That's good said I, you must be happy that he's doing the job at last,
She stared at me and then at Ken and her expression was aghast.
Happy, said Celia, he's useless; he's nothing but a joke
Without covering the carpets and settee what's a matter with the bloke.

I tried to point out Ken's good points to ease the atmosphere
But it would be easier learning Russian, I must get out of here.
Now Kenneth in his wisdom went to put the kettle on
And in the lounge sat Celia looking daggers across at Ron.
He tries his best, does Ken, said I with my tongue in my cheek
He must have done something right at some time during this week.

I did the shopping yesterday said Ken whilst carrying cups and biscuit jar
Shopping said she, you dropped me of at Morrison's and never left the car.
While we had our refreshments Celia's mood lightened up a lot
And as we talked about her paintings the happier she got.
I'll make some picture frames tomorrow said Ken who now sat on the floor
It was then I made my swift exit out of their wooden back door.

The Walking Group

The walking group meets every week
And set out from the local church.
Past rows of houses and into fields
Past mighty oaks and silver birch
Natures wonders for to seek.

Through woods and fields we boldly go
In summer sun and winter snow.
Tony in front and Karen behind
And other walk leaders of every kind
Walking for pleasure, bringing peace of mind.

A lively group of like minded friends
The lively chatter as they walk along.
Through countryside they wander on
See squirrels at play and birds at song
The joy they feel should never end.

To bird sanctuary or country park
This motley crew by car embark.
Along footpaths by canal and stream
To reservoir and sculpture park
And stop for tea or Walls' ice cream.

The benefits to health are great
A fact we often celebrate.
To see natures wonders as we walk
Through fields and woods or Barker's Park
We all agree we're glad to be
The walking group of Kimbewworth Park.

Cherry Wine and a Gladstone Bag

I used to have a Gladstone bag in which to keep my tools
I bought it from a Yorkshire lass, who used to teach in schools.
I met her while on a camping holiday which simply was divine
She was with a friend called Alice and they were drunk on cherry wine.

She stumbled across the campsite with her legs all wobbly and bent
And she tripped over a guy rope and fell into the warden's tent.
The lantern fell on the ground and the centre pole did sag
She fell over backwards upon her Gladstone bag.

She said her bag was too heavy and had caused her embarrassing fall
But if you knew that wicked lady you would not believe that at all.
She sold the Gladstone bag next day to a sober man named Ron
To keep his bits and pieces in, in safety, from that sad day on.

Her friend called Alice was also drunk on cherry wine just then,
She was famous throughout Yorkshire for sketching naked men.
Back at the tent she spied poor Ron and gave him such a fright,
"I'm sleeping with my clothes on" he said, "You're not drawing me tonight".

The rest of my holiday simply was eventful to say the very least.
To drink bottles of cherry wine with fish and chips certainly was a feast.
The two ladies became the best of friends and I know this may be a shock
They drink coffee with my wife and I each week at one O'clock.

Printed in Great Britain
by Amazon

24098686R00036